BURNING BEACONS [REMASTERED]

RAJIV R NAIR & R. S. CHINTALAPATI

Dedicated to
Resmi Ravindran & Parvati Chintalapati

Contents

Sex

A newly married couple discuss the possible gender of their child to realize that they have different choices. While agreeing that a healthy child is a common request, they are also surprised to realize they disagree on the name considering their differences in opinion on characters from epics.

CHAPTER ONE

DAY 0

As the cold winds swirled into the room through the open window, Bhaskar looked at his wife as he felt her for the first time. He could tell she was controlling her pain but her eyes were filled with tears. Unable to witness her agony, he pulled himself out of her and when he did, he could feel her bleeding.

He looked at her for a moment as she took a deep breath. A moment later, he leaned forward and kissed her. As she kissed him back, tears rolled down her eyes as she closed them. The nineteen-year-old Radha, he married a day ago, caressed his black curly hair after they kissed.

Looking into her eyes, Bhaskar could see her willingness before he felt her again. For a while, the couple moaned in pleasure before he passed the life gifted to him.

As he did, he truly felt the transcendence of power within and it was like never before and as she received it, she ushered in joyful pain looking at the man whom she chose to lead her life with.

Taking a deep breath, Bhaskar rested on his wife's bosom feeling her heart pace. He felt the wait was worth every minute and life has never been more complete.

Feeling his warmth, Radha asked, "What would you wish the Gods for? A boy or a girl?"

Placing his chin between her life preservers, Bhaskar replied, "I would like to welcome Saraswati. What about you?"

With a smile, Radha replied, "I wish for a girl too. It would be like my elder sister being reborn."

Recalling how the lack of medical facilities led to her ten-year-old sister die of sickness, Radha curiously asked, "What if the Gods give you a son?"

Thinking about it for a moment, Bhaskar teased, "Looks like madam would, after all, prefer a son."

Glancing at her husband, Radha laughed before confessing, "It was my father's wish. He wanted a grandson named Arjun. Though I would love a daughter, I would prefer a boy equally, too."

Leaning forward, Bhaskar stated, "Arjun? Rather than name our son of an overrated protagonist, I would name him of a fallen antagonist."

Finishing his sentence, Bhaskar kissed his wife on her neck. When they looked into each other's eyes, Radha replied, "My husband should certainly read Mahabharat once again.

Maybe then, he wouldn't root for the fallen and realize the reason behind such a fate."

Listening to her, Bhaskar just smiled. He knew she wasn't completely wrong.

A moment later, he mentioned, "Honestly Radha, it doesn't matter who it is. I just hope they are born healthy and continue our bloodline with at least the respect we hold now."

Radha couldn't be more glad. Her husband's words gave her more pleasure than their actions.

Meanwhile, Bhaskar lied on her bosom and closed his eyes before falling asleep. Caressing his hair, Radha closed her eyes too.

For a while, she could see a man in his thirties standing behind them while three young children were playing before them on the floor while she sat beside her husband posing for a picture.

She lived the moment for a few seconds before losing it.

Death

When not a single person in this world cares about another's existence, the motivation to live for a socially dependent person ceases. The lawfully unaccepted notion of ending one's own life doesn't seem to be a choice but rather a destination. The misery of the mental self is strikingly dangerous with unforeseen consequences when not controlled.

CHAPTER TWO

DAY 15,702

Placing his plate of warm noodles on the dining table, Radheya recalled Mitram. He thought about how Mitram would have stopped him before he tasted his unusually sweet noodles.

Though he thought of taking a look at the portraits of all those whom he loved, Radheya started stuffing noodles into his mouth without wasting another moment. When he finished his noodles, he felt nothing.

It took a few moments before the intended reaction kicked in. While he was experiencing the pain, Radheya recalled about the online friend he invited for dinner. Observing the clock, he knew that she wouldn't even arrive for the next twenty minutes.

Moments before his mortal form lost its soul, Radheya couldn't help but think, "Why did I even strive in life if this is how it would have ended?"

More than pain, Radheya dreaded the thought of what would happen next. He was certain about Gods and demons being nothing more than mere elements of the mind and firmly disagreed on their existence in the fictional concept of the afterlife. However, when facing death, the uncertainty certainly terrified him.

As he pondered on the question, the doorbell buzzed. Glancing at the clock in the dining room, Radheya couldn't help but presume that his guest arrived early. Trying to look calm, he walked to the door as he felt the pain in his stomach.

Looking through the peephole, he saw his friend standing steady. He opened the unlocked door to find a stunning girl in her late twenties wearing a black gown standing before him.

As his eyes closed, Radheya mentioned, "You're early…"

Observing her getting tense, he raised his hand in assurance before he crashed on the floor. The moment he crashed, he could see his astral form still standing.

As his body landed on the floor, the girl just stood there for a moment. She could see he wasn't breathing and just calmly left. He was surprised that she didn't even call the police as he had expected.

An hour later, one of his neighbors noticed him lying at the entrance and called the emergency services. A couple of hours later, Radheya's mortal form was before a drunk surgeon whose quest was to find what killed him.

Though the intoxicated mortal knew that even the

strongest leaf shall have to fall when kissed by winter, he was just checking the math of self-killers. Even he knew that the world he lived in was filled with no emotional entailment and just survived on rational investments alone.

After the inspector determined that the corpse owner killed himself, Radheya was surprised to see his body parts were being snatched to be reused. The rest of the poisoned filth was packed into a black bag like a broken toy before being shipped on a conveyor belt that carried many other bodies.

Another officer took a look at the tag on the bag before marking it in his system. In absolute silence, the conveyor belt passed the body into the incarceration chamber and burnt Radheya's body instantly.

Radheya could see the mortal form that he built for four decades turn into ashes in seconds. As he believed, neither angels nor demons awaited. It was the darkness that surrounded him as he always stated. In such silence, he knew not a single living soul was weeping for him.

Birth

Feeling a newborn for the first time is an experience that's unparalleled. Especially when that life is related. It's like feeling God in mortal form by those corrupted by materialism during their course of existence.

CHAPTER THREE

DAY 283

Picking up the transmitter, Bhaskar's manager accepted his request to meet him. After signing a few documents, he waved at Bhaskar to enter the chamber.

He waved again listening to Bhaskar's plea and Bhasker immediately rushed on his scooter to the hospital. Enquiring his wife's name at the information center, he rushed to the maternity ward where he found his wife unconscious.

Walking towards the cradle beside the bed, Bhaskar could see his spitting image sleeping in silence. Happiness filled his eyes with tears as he extended his hand to touch him.

Looking at his son laying in the cradle, Bhaskar's mother mentioned, "The Gods have given you an heir!"

Observing her son staring at the life he sourced, she continued, "Lakshmi will soon join."

No matter what his mother said, Bhaskar couldn't take his eyes off the beautiful life that was before him. He knew there was a reason henceforth to strive and without a second thought, he promised himself that all his actions should serve his little one.

The moment he felt him, tears of happiness slid his cheek as his mother hugged him.

Touching his adorable finger, Bhaskar mentioned, "It's him."

With a smile, his mother acknowledged, "He couldn't be away for long considering how much you loved him."

Meanwhile, Srinivas stood before Rudra, staring at his third eye. Staring at the inordinate amount of energy, Srinivas asked, "Why was I summoned, father?"

With a charismatic smile, Rudra replied, "You shall have to relive another dharmic life in-order to become a part of me, child."

Kneeling, Srinivas begged, "Forgive my sins father. I do not wish to live in that hell. I would rather take any other punishment. Please don't send me again..."

Continuing to smile, Rudra mentioned, "You haven't been cleansed yet, child. Your desires should be destroyed before you become a part of me. You were created from me for that specific purpose."

Accepting his fate, Srinivas pleaded, "At least give me strength father!"

For one last time, Srinivas saw Rudra before being thrown into darkness. He heard nothing but then, he heard his wife and son.

He felt delighted that the almighty had decided for him to be born into the same family, but before long he had no recollection of them anymore.

As Bhaskar turned to look at his wife, his mother asked, "Are you planning to name him Srinivas?"

Not intending to lie, Bhaskar replied, "Not until I saw him. I always wanted him to be Karna."

With a smile, his mother replied, "Since fallen heroes are today's icons and distorted comprehension of epics cannot be undone. Taking his mother's name into account, let's name him Radheya."

Silence prevailed for a moment before she continued, "You could have your wish. Just name him Radheya instead of Karna."

After a moment of thought, Bhaskar suggested, "If it is Radheya, then let it be Srinivas Radheya."

Life

Continuing to devote time to elements that aren't believable is an unquestioned activity though tiring. Such activities make even the lamest individuals question their motives as time passes by. However, the cost of giving up is often based on the emotional value held on them.

CHAPTER FOUR

DAY 14,775

On a cloudy morning, Radheya opened his car door for Mitram to get in and after cautiously closing the door, he rushed to the driver's seat.

Turning the key, Radheya mentioned, "I know you would want the window open but it's too cold and you can enjoy nature as long as you want in the park."

The Indian Spitz just stared at its master in silence as they drove. Just like any other Saturday, Mitram presumed that they would first go to a park and then shop before returning home.

A few lanes later, Radheya took a turn that wasn't usually their route. Noticing Mitram raising his ears, Radheya assured, "We are going to the Shiva temple."

For a moment, silence prevailed before Radheya justified, "My father wanted me to feed him after his death. You could just say it was his dying wish."

Rushing to the nearby Shiva temple, Radheya parked his car

and opened Mitram's door before paying the parking fee to a boy. Requesting him to take care of his dog, Radheya tied the leash to a nearby pole before entering the temple.

Paying at the shoe locker, Radheya thought, "Why shouldn't dogs be permitted into temples? Aren't they a creation of God?"

Stepping into the temple premises barefooted, Radheya had to follow the queue that led to the taps. Authorities insisted that visitors wash their feet before they stepped into the temple premises.

The more time he had to stay in the queue, Radheya grew more restless of having left Mitram outside. However, neither could he break the line nor control his thoughts.

Getting his feet wet, he rushed to the Puskarini to find someone he could pay to get the job done.

At the same time, in the world of the Eternals, the doors of the Immortal Lands opened and Radha's spirit walked out along with many others to accept offerings made to her if any.

Though she kind of knew that she wouldn't be offered food, not giving up hope, Radha requested an astral crow to fetch her if any food was offered.

Meeting the first priest on the stairs leading to the puskarini, Radheya asked, "Would you offer food on my behalf to my father if I pay you?"

Taking a look at the healthy man in his forties, the priest replied, "I wouldn't."

Without an argument, Radheya moved to the next priest and asked the same question, and this time a deal was made. While paying the second priest after giving him the details, the first priest mentioned, "Spare a few minutes for your parents' child. They will be content with your offering."

Without a word or expressing anger on those who lie in the name of God, Radheya left. Rushing towards Mitram, he untied the leash and apologized twice before hugging the dog.

Meanwhile, the astral crow heard the chanting of mantras before arriving at the Shiva temple. It could see that the priest who had taken up the task offered nothing more than just water.

Picking up a drop of water through its beak, it returned to Radha. On its way, it saw Mitram and for a moment, Mitram noticed him before howling.

Noticing the crow returning alongside a million others, Radha hoped she would be fed after such a long time but soon enough, she got to know she had to stay hungry for another day just like most of her companions.

Returning to the hall, Radha ate the last morsel of the fruit given by Rudra.

Afterlife

Fighting and killing in the name of a force that is questioned to even exist shouldn't even be an option. At times, it seems ludicrous to end lives under the presumption of serving or defending the unseen master. This however, shouldn't force the non-believers to condemn others who abide by laws of the master guiding them.

CHAPTER FIVE

DAY 7,300

On a sunny day, sitting behind his father, Radheya was reading the news on his phone listening to the priest chant Sanskrit slokas. He didn't comprehend a word of what was recited and he was least interested.

While swiping the local news, Radheya read, 'A Man killed in the name of God!'

For a moment when Radheya couldn't control himself. He didn't know who should be blamed for this? The rigid mindsets of the elders who force Gods on their children or the rebelling youngsters who want to overthrow a system they don't understand.

Looking around him, he saw the temple and not intending to continue being a hypocrite, he stood up and left without saying a word. While the priest observed him, he didn't stop his chants.

Completing the offering, Bhaskar touched the feet of the priest before returning to his car. He could see Radheya resting beside his mother.

Placing his angavastram in the front seat, Bhaskar controlled his anger and pleasantly questioned, "Why did you leave?"

Without a moment of hesitation and neglecting all of his mother's advice, Radheya replied, "Couldn't believe how you were being tricked by a priest. Didn't want myself to be tricked too."

Following his words, Radha asked, "Would you keep your mouth shut?"

Raising his hand to gesture to his wife to remain calm, Bhaskar enquired, "You think our forefathers aren't waiting for us to feed them?"

Disappointed, Radheya replied, "There is no such thing as an afterlife father! It's a folly that is run by tax-evading businessmen."

While Radha was shocked, Bhaskar smirked before asking, "What about Gods? Do they even exist?"

Radheya could see his mother getting emotional as he said, "Gods are elements created by humans in order to maintain order in an otherwise chaotic society."

Disgusted, Bhaskar asked, "You think God is a tool of fear rather than a Creator?"

With a smirk, Radheya replied, "If there is an Almighty, then he or she shall have to be prosecuted for overseeing so many catastrophic events and doing little to nothing."

As soon as Radheya finished his sentence, Bhaskar realized it's too late to even teach his son. Controlling his anger and sorrow, he started the car and they rode home.

That afternoon while eating lunch, Bhaskar asked, "Can I ask you if you would offer us food after we die?"

His question was immediately followed by Radha shouting, "Enough of it for today!"

With her instructions, silence prevailed over the topic forever. However, Bhaskar always feared the consequences of such bad parenting even when Radha assured, "It's not our fault. It's the time we live in."

While Bhaskar disagreed by stating, "Our knowledge is no longer a path to wisdom but is rather a defense for our ignorance. It has nothing to do with the times."

He couldn't help but agree that Gods have become obsolute and the few with their intellect and motivation are striving to nullify their mere existence. While others are using them for vile ambitions and create blind followers.

Afterlife

When answering metaphysical questions most often individuals are left to find logical conclusions through rigorous learning and discussions. Such a process could at times provide a visualization of achieving completeness in life. However, what disrupts such a journey from being complete is the desire to acquire validation from peers.

CHAPTER SIX

DAY 10,950

On a cloudy evening after their class, Supriya and Radheya decided to complete their evening routine before returning to their room.

After collecting drinks from the vending machine, Supriya sipped her tea before asking, "So you're telling me that heaven and hell exist theoretically."

Observing his coffee drip into the cup, Radheya replied, "Yes, in the minds of those who believe in them."

Walking to an empty table for two in the cafeteria, Supriya replied, "I think it's a well-crafted fantasy tale to establish order amongst humans."

Sipping on his sweetened coffee, Radheya agreed before stating, "Imagine having no payoff when you die even after leading a life following every rule set before you."

For a moment, Supriya didn't say a word and Radheya waited until she asked, "What if they are right? What if there is heaven and hell? What if we are wrong?"

With a smirk, Radheya replied, "I'll be in hell before I would even realize I'm dead."

Sipping her lukewarm tea, Supriya replied, "Worry not, I will be just behind you."

With a smile, Radheya asked, "Do you think humans are still eligible to go to heaven in this messed up world?"

Supriya just nodded in disagreement before stating, "I think our belief system could be validated on the premise that the existence of a supernatural force like God who doesn't respond is a flawed design. The early humans feared everything beyond their control and declared them to be divine beings before starting to worship them."

Looking into her black eyes, Radheya pointed out, "Of course they would worship them. If they wouldn't please them, these forces could destroy these tiny beings within no time. Imagine being eaten by the sea, burnt by the Sun, torn by the wind, or being drenched by the rain."

Amused, Supriya continued, "It baffles me that people, even now, think these prayers work. Even after such scientific progress, do they seriously think Devas are resting in their thrones receiving our prayers? I don't know how they believe that praying to these unseen forces could save us as a race."

Looking at the grey clouds, Radheya pointed, "Fear forces people to do illogical things and the divine is one such force of fear."

Holding hands, Supriya mentioned, "Our children should be given the choice rather than be forced like us."

With a smile, Radheya mentioned, "I'm sure they would believe in Gods. The new generation is being fed in such a way that Gods are going to be their all-time companions. A war between the radicals on both sides is inevitable eventually."

Finishing her tea, Supriya replied, "Let's see how many messengers and avatars would come to our rescue."

Placing their cups on the conveyor belt, they started walking towards their room.

As they walked, Radheya mentioned, 'My mother wants us to get married."

Controlling her laughter, Supriya replied, "Didn't you tell her that I let you have me without the holy thread?"

With a smile, Radheya replied, "You will get me into trouble someday."

Life

If there is a single reality in the face of death, shouldn't every individual either start an afterlife or just stop existing. However, such absolute ends are often questioned when talking about mind travel or astral forms. When pondering about existing on the other side of the portal, death is just the beginning of an individual's journey to the worlds they believed in throughout their lifetime.

CHAPTER SEVEN

DAY 12,410

Into the darkness, as the Sun faded and shadows grew, Radheya stood at the front along with his cousin holding the cot that held his father's corpse.

Bhaskar's mortal eyes were closed and on the top of his body floated his soul watching the procession. He could see people mourning but couldn't feel it personally and as the four men representative of the four servants of the death bringer took him to be fed to the fire, Bhaskar relished in joy seeing the angels floating in the sky. They were the lights in the unending darkness.

Like the four men who held his mortal form, there were four angels who stood around his pyre waiting for the funeral rites to be completed.

Their rhythmic moves swung his mortal form on the cot and the chantings of the holy men kept the wild spirits away.

Looking at them trying to grab him into their darkness terrified Bhaskar. It seemed as if they hated the light and wouldn't let a soul walk to the heavens while they suffered in their unending darkness striving to live once more.

As his mortal form was approaching the pyre, Bhaskar rejoiced until he heard Radha scream miles away.

Nothing pained him until this point but her sorrow made him want to live again. There wasn't him without her and there wasn't her without him.

He could see that she was running towards the graveyard even when women were prohibited. Bhaskar's soul wanted to stop her.

Turning towards the four angels, Bhaskar pleaded, "Stop her!"

They didn't move. This time talking to Mother Nature, Bhaskar pleaded again and the black clouds poured down along with cold winds.

At the center of the mortal and Eternals, prayers were offered before Radheya set his father's corpse on fire. As the angels approached to hold Bhaskar's soul, they could see Radha jumping into the pyre in absolute silence while no one even saw her coming.

They could see her smile as her saree got torched and her flesh burnt. Without even shouting once in pain, the fire ate her while she died glancing at her son in her final moments.

Everyone was aghast and before they could react, she was gone forever.

Seeing the woman kill herself, all souls from the darkness rushed towards her. For the sinners shall always be with them.

Observing the souls rushing towards them, two of the four angels created their trishuls and the souls stopped at a distance.

As Bhaskar held Radha, she just smiled looking at him. After all, their belief was true indeed. The angels smiled looking at them before they opened the gates for the stairs that took them to the Gods.

Ascending the stairs, the couple entered a chamber following the angels to see millions of souls eating alongside Rudra. They picked the fruits from Kalpavriksham - a tree that stood like an umbrella above them.

Looking at them, Rudra stood up to approach them and they just bowed. While the couple looked stunning, he mentioned, "Times have changed children. Grab a few fruits."

Observing them not moving, Rudra stated, "Radha, go grab some fruits. I wouldn't like you to stay hungry."

Without a second thought, Radha left while Bhaskar didn't move his sight an inch. Turning to him, Rudra mentioned, "You have lived a dutiful life Bhaskar but you shall have to be reborn."

Thinking about another life, Bhaskar couldn't help but frown. Looking at him, Rudra mentioned, "You shall have to live your karma before becoming a part of me."

For a moment, silence prevailed before Rudra assured, "It shall not be for a long time. You shall not be a human this time but shall rather be his companion."

As soon as Rudra concluded, Radha returned with four fruits. Taking a fruit from her, Rudra replied, "You need to reap the fruits of what you have sown Bhaskar. You need to see what you have done."

While Radha wondered what happened, Bhaskar knew it was his offspring that Rudra was talking about.

With a smile, the almighty replied, "You will soon be a part of me, my child. This shall be your last life."

Bhaskar smiled while Radha couldn't help but begin to plead.

Birth

Time and loneliness turn even the most intelligent insane. In societies where bondings are feeble and belief systems are introspected to the extent of causing disbelief, dependencies between individuals become impractical. However, living in a world of the void is as good as non-existing, and seeking to love other forms of life who could be partners is no longer an alternative.

CHAPTER EIGHT

DAY 13,510

Filling up the documentation, Radheya took a look at the Indian Spitz that was soon going to be his family member.

After finalizing the payments and the first checkup of his place to verify if he could provide the dog a good home, Radheya was given permission to adopt.

Finishing the form, Radheya took hold of the dog leash. With a smile on his face of having owned a loyal lifelong companion, Radheya walked out of the store to find many others like him.

As he walked in the sunset, Radheya said, "Hey Mitram, you must take good care of me. It's you and me kid. We aren't left with anyone who could offer us a long term commitment."

For a moment, Radheya looked at the cute dog before presuming he heard him. After taking a few steps, Radheya continued, "I don't know what I'm supposed to do but at this age, I cannot take another betrayal and I promise not to betray you. I will stay loyal. The last time I did that to

Supriya, she didn't just walk away but even returned the favor."

Both of them walked home while Mitram heard his master. It took a few moments before Radheya mentioned, "My intellectual mother, my saintly father, and my loyal partner fucked up my life.... You're the only one I could rely on."

They walked and Mitram rejoiced in the cold air as well as its freedom. However, the chain still held him. He could figure out that his master has more issues than it seemed.

Meanwhile Radheya continued, "I hope she comes back. I hope she understands that it's just the heat of the moment that I cheated on her."

The very next moment he stated, "When she cheated on me, I never questioned. How come she gets to judge me?"

Listening to his master, Mitram could sense that darkness filled him. He thought, "How should I send him to therapy?"

Recalling the days when he was trained, Mitram thought, "So this is one in the most intellectual race? A bitter man having a psychological breakdown yet pretending his best."

While he was lost in his thoughts, Mitram heard Radheya confess, "Even now, if she returns, I will take her back."

Mitram couldn't comprehend his thoughts and the rest of their journey, Radheya told him about the first time he met Supriya. When they reached home, Mitram could see video game decals, popstar posters, fashionable skulls, and lots of empty bottles.

He knew the journey had just begun. Either he would be dragged into the darkness or bring back light into Radheya's life. The herculean task of reviving his master would be his goal.

Death

Does torturing sinners change them? Can bad deeds be corrected with punishment? Then doesn't it beg the question as to why individuals are created to be later punished by the very Gods from whom they have taken a form? Do sinners have to be stuck in the cycle of unending lives until they satisfy the standards set by the eternal beings?

CHAPTER NINE

DAY 15,695

Entering the garden of life, Radha followed the guards of Rudra as they led the way. The floating trees that grew on clouds represented every family that existed in human life.

As the two guards reached Eluri's tree, Radha could see a dying tree. Worried, she asked, "Is there a way one can protect it from dying?"

Both the guards just started walking and without paying heed took her to her second family tree, this time the tree was dead. Staring at it, Radha couldn't speak a word.

After a moment of silence, one of the guards mentioned, "The cycle of life dictates that even the most powerful element existing shall fall prey. None of us can stop or change it. All we can do is learn to live with it."

Still glancing at the tree, Radha asked, "So shall I presume that my maternal line has ended?"

With a smile, the other guard replied, "In a cycle, nothing ends. It's either on the top or on the bottom. For every leaf that is dropping now, one more shall take its place. An imbalance is never a constraint. It is only a few of those who perceive it to be one."

Following him, the first guard mentioned, "It's true. Your son shall be the last of your family by blood but the family name shall live on through others."

Thinking about her son for a moment, Radha asked, "Will I see him again?"

Staring at each other for a moment, one of the guards mentioned, "You might. However, if he doesn't believe in God, then we cannot help him."

Doubtful if she heard it right, Radha asked, "An atheist doesn't even belong in hell?"

Her question made both the guards smile. Noticing her sincere appeal, a guard replied, "God doesn't punish non-believers. It is not even the least of their intentions."

Following him, the second guard mentioned, "The non-believers are left in the void. They are left to what they believe in. Souls have the power to choose their afterlife and if they firmly believe in something after death, it's highly likely they will end up there."

Anxious, Radha stated, "My son doesn't believe in God. What shall happen to him? Please don't tell me he would be left in the void."

Both the guards didn't say a word but just started walking

away and Radha understood the answer wasn't complicated.

Sex

If individuals have the power to create life while experiencing sexual pleasure, doesn't it corrupt the weak to waste it for their own? Should individuals be punished for such corrupted nature? If punished, who should pass such a judgment, if the existence of the supreme is presumed annulled?

CHAPTER TEN

DAY 15,695

It has been thirty hours since Radheya slept. Even if he tried, he couldn't listen to Mitram wail in pain. He knew it's time to say goodbye and Radheya held him while both of them slept on their comfy bed.

Looking at Mitram asleep, Radheya recalled the doctor's words about losing Mitram soon before he closed his eyes. For an unknown reason, he recalled the first time he met Supriya.

A dorm party welcoming freshers. It was the first time most of the students met and after a couple of hours, when everyone introduced themselves, the first game began.

The ping pong game where you throw the ping pong ball into a glass to have a shot. While Radheya sucked at it, Supriya rocked.

She won so many rounds that she was filled with tequila. After the first game, there was some free time and Radheya approached her to ask her name.

The moment she informed me of her name, she mentioned, "If you have any other intentions than just flirting, my dorm is nearby."

For a moment, Radheya couldn't believe she said that. Looking at him, she teased, "I know how much time it would take you to get to me and I'm done pretending that I love the way you choose your words."

He couldn't help but smile and she continued, "So let me make it clear. I like the way you look and I suppose you do too and I'm sure this wouldn't go any further than tonight."

Looking into her black eyes, Radheya mentioned, "We never know. It might."

Smiling back, she replied, "I know. It won't."

The next moment, she held his hand and both of them left the party. Entering her dorm, they dropped the keys, ripped each other's clothes off and he felt her tongue sliding over his and admittedly, she was the best one until this point. Controlling himself, Radheya wore his companion before he rode her from the top.

She smiled wickedly and it drove him crazy. So, he punished her by racing like a horse. Though she shouted along with him, he still couldn't wipe the smile off her face.

Flipping her like a coin, he pierced into her while the smile on her face faded. Holding her black hair with golden strands, he humped like a dog until the life within reached its pinnacle upon which he stood up while Supriya sat beneath him feeling the lukewarm power touch her face.

The moment her smile reappeared, Radheya opened his eyes. He couldn't feel Mitram's life and what was thrown away never returned when needed.

About Contributors

1. **Rajiv R Nair**

   Rajiv has been a member of the community since 2015 and he writes flash fiction & short stories. His works can be accessed at writerspouch.com/profile/24

2. **R. S. Chintalapati**

   Ravi is the founder of the community and he writes short stories & clicks pictures. His works can be accessed at writerspouch.com/profile/2

About Editors

1. **Ahna Sahi**

   Ahna has been a member of the community since 2017 and she edits non-fiction and novels. Her edited works can be accessed at writerspouch.com/profile/30

2. **Sree Raj**

   Sree has been a member of the community since 2011 and he edits non-fiction and novels alongside writing poems. His edited works can be accessed at writerspouch.com/profile/4

3. **Tarun Chintam**

   Tarun has been a member of the community since 2017 and he edits novelettes, novellas and novels. His edited works can be accessed at writerspouch.com/profile/29

About Photographer

Pankaj Tottada

Pankaj has been a member of the community since 2015 and he has contributed numerous photographs. His contributions can be accessed at writerspouch.com/profile/13

About Community

Writers Pouch is an art community that commissions various works of different art forms. Encompassing creators, contributors, editors, proofreaders, reviewers, photographers, and illustrators, the organisation aims to create unique forms of art in every genre.

Established in 2009, Writers Pouch started by publishing short stories, essays and poems. Later on, the organisation even started releasing novelettes, novellas, novels, book series, & non-fiction.

The goal of Writers Pouch is to explore art uniquely and this is accomplished by commissioning a group of artists on every project. They are a home for all creative individuals who are striving to tell their stories or ideas creatively while holding on to their principles.

If you loved our works, visit our website at writerspouch.com to buy our other titles.

1. I'm Your Loving Intern [2015]
2. Loving Intern [2016]
3. The Soul Snatchers [2016]
4. Broken Bonds [2017]
5. God's Council: The Four Auins [2017]
6. Your Loving Intern [2018]
7. Eternal Love [2019]